For my lovely
Bridesmaid
Thanks.
Catherine
Elliott x
—S.H.

For my
wonderful
editor, Anne
—S.L.J.

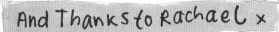

And Thanks to Rachael x

E
375-6718

I ♡ my
dog
x

Published by Schwartz & Wade Books
an imprint of Random House Children's Books
a division of Random House, Inc., New York

Text copyright © 2009 by Sally Lloyd-Jones
Illustrations copyright © 2009 Sue Heap
All rights reserved.

Schwartz & Wade Books and colophon are trademarks of Random House, Inc.

Visit us on the Web! www.randomhouse.com/kids
Educators and librarians, for a variety of teaching tools,
visit us at www.randomhouse.com/teachers

Library of Congress Cataloging-in-Publication Data
Lloyd-Jones, Sally.
How to get married—by me, the bride / Sally Lloyd-Jones ; illustrated by Sue Heap.—
1st ed.
p. cm.
Summary: An all-knowing little girl teaches her friends how to get married,
from picking the right mate to getting engaged to dancing at the wedding.

ISBN 978-0-375-84118-7 (trade) — ISBN 978-0-375-94118-4 (lib. bdg.)
[1. Marriage—Fiction. 2. Humorous stories.] I. Heap, Sue, ill. II. Title.

PZ7.L77878Hr 2009
[E]—dc22
2007037839

The text of this book is set in Stempel Garamond.
The illustrations are rendered in acrylic paint,
crayons, and a 0.7-millimeter felt-tip pen.
Book design by Rachael Cole.

PRINTED IN CHINA
10 9 8 7 6 5 4 3 2 1
First Edition

How to Get Married by Me, the Bride

and Sally Lloyd-Jones
and Sue Heap

schwartz & wade books · new york

W
hen you want to get married,
first you have to find someone you can marry.

You can marry your best friend
or your teacher
or your pet
or your daddy.
(And sometimes you can marry a flower.)

You can marry someone who is just like you,
or someone who isn't,

someone who lives near your house,
or someone who doesn't.

Actually, you can marry anyone you like!
(Except they need to like you back.)

When you are choosing a Husband or a Wife,
you have to be on your best behavior.
You can't be mean. You have to be nice.
For instance, no one will want to marry you
if you gobble up all their candy
and never offer them any.

Or if you pick your nose in front of them.
Or pinch them.
And you shouldn't yawn when they are talking to you
or you will hurt their feelings
and they won't want to see you ever again.

BASICALLY, NO ONE WILL MARRY YOU IF:

* You wear old pajamas and slippers in the middle of the day

! You don't EVER take a bath

☆ You don't EVER brush your hair and it looks like a bird's nest back there

‼ You dribble your dinner down your chin

Usually, you're not allowed to marry
lots of people at once.
Except sometimes you are.

And NEVER get married when it's dark
because you won't be able to see
and you might marry the wrong person.

But not EVERYONE is good to marry.
If you marry a cat, for instance,
you have to let him lick your face.

If you marry a teacher,
she could make you do homework
instead of watch TV.

If you marry a noisy shouting person,
he will give you a headache.
And if you marry a firefighter,
you have to let him practice
on you and not say, "Cut it out!"

! Someone too big or they won't fit in your house

* Someone too small or you might squash Your Husband by mistake

!! Someone who only eats bugs. YUCK!

Sometimes you have to search and search
for the right person
and travel far and wide
until you find them.
And sometimes you just have to sit quietly
and wait for someone.

When you have found your Own True Love,
you must ask their permission.

"Can I marry you, please?" you say.
"Yes, please," they say.

And you say, "Thank you very much,"
and do your best curtsy or bow
and kneel down and give them a golden ring
or your favorite toy
or a bite of your cookie.
And that means you're allowed to get married.

From now on, you say, "Sweetheart, where are you, My Sweetheart?"

and "My Honey Darling, look at me, My Honey!" and stuff like that (so everyone knows they're yours and won't try to marry them too).

Next you send out all the invitations
so your friends can come and see you get married.
You must write in beautiful Wedding Language

Please come to our wedding
because we kindly request
the pleasure of your company.
There will be candy.
RSVP

and put "RSVP" at the end
(which is French and means
Please Say Yes Please Thank You).

Now you need to find a Special Wedding Place.

HERE ARE SOME GOOD PLACES TO GET MARRIED:
* A big white tent
♡ A palace

It's very important to wear something beautiful for your wedding.

FOR EXAMPLE, YOU COULD WEAR:

* A pure white dress like the moon
♥ Some shining armor
✓ A mustache
! Some wings if you are a Fairy Bride

And it's nice if you put something romantic on top of your head.
Like a long veil, for instance.

HERE'S WHAT ELSE COULD GO ON YOUR HEAD:
- ✔ A crown
- ✔ A wig
- ✱ !Some ears in case you're marrying a rabbit

Your friends and sisters and pets and toys and grandmas
should all come to see your wedding in their best outfits.
And when the music starts
everyone has to stop WHATEVER
they're doing and look at you.

And you walk down the aisle,
which means you must go extra slowly
down a long path
and not fall over.

Next, you stand very still,
and look right in each other's faces.
And you say, "I do!"
And they say, "I do, too!"

Then someone with an Important Voice says,
"I now pronounce you Husband and Wife!"

And that means you are married.

Now you throw a big bunch of flowers
at people's heads.
It's called the bouquet, and whoever it hits
has to get married next.

Everyone shouts and jumps up in the air
and throws snow at you
(except it's called confetti and it's only pretend).

And your guests have to hand over TONS of presents
and give you a big cake with LOTS of frosting on it
and sing you a wedding song
and be so happy they could cry.

And your smile is nearly jumping off your face.

AND THEN HERE'S WHAT YOU HAVE
TO DO NEXT :

☆   Let everyone take your picture

♡   Open all the presents

✳   eat up all the cake

☆   and dance a little Wedding Dance

And now you are Married People.
So you have to yell, "HOORAY!"
and then do some cartwheels for joy.

HERE'S WHAT ELSE MARRIED PEOPLE HAVE TO DO:

* ✳ Get some children (maybe) and some pets (definitely)
* ☆ Live in a house on a hill by a little stream
* ♡ Watch the sun go down
* ✳ Go along together holding hands
* ☆ Live Happily Ever After THE END

Except first you have to say goodbye to your guests.
"Goodbye, Guests!" you must say.
Then you wave and skip all the way home,
and hold your daddy's hand,
and give him a bite of your cake,
and show him your presents,
and tell him all about your very completely lovely
Happily-Ever-After Wedding.

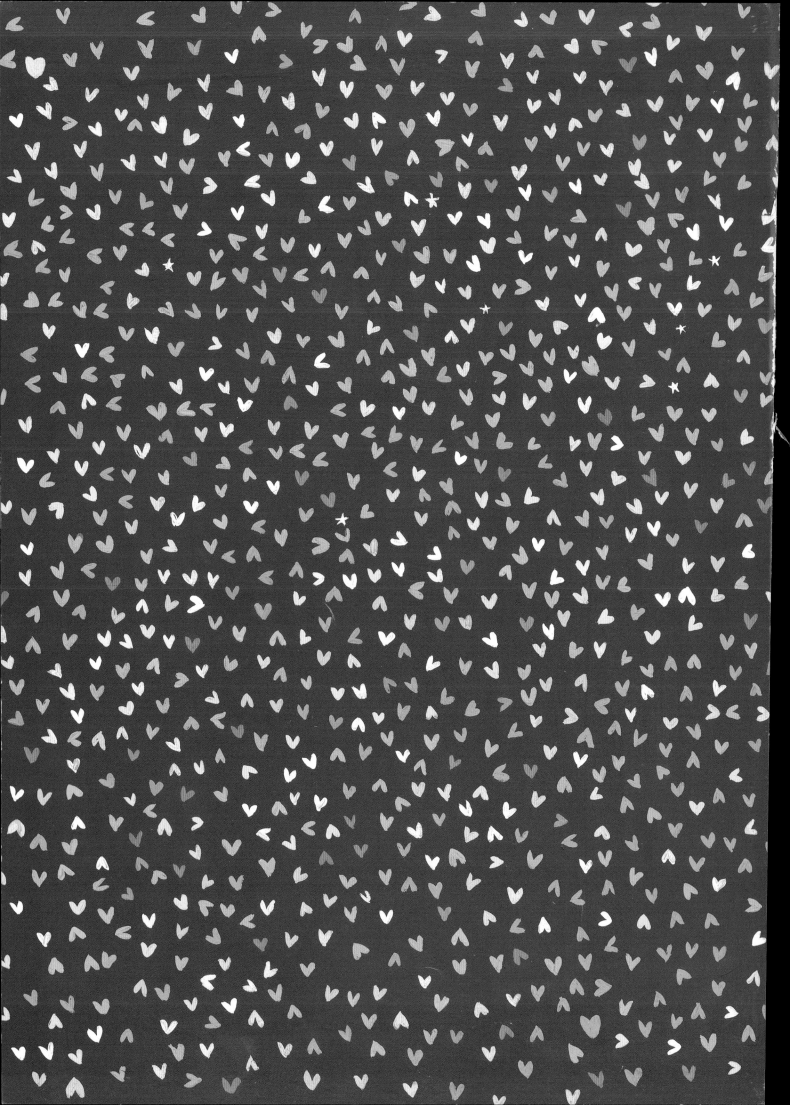